insane., cool history of iCarly. iCarly has officially blown up! And, no, I don't mean that my brother, Spencer, put a metal container of leftover Chinese take-out in the microwave and blew up our studio—I mean the show is reaching tons of viewers! We knew our friends and kids from school would watch, but now it's spread way beyond Seattle.

I guess being a Web star has its ups and downs (I hope the "ups" include a lifetime supply of free smoothies at Groovy Smoothie. Mmm . . .). We have fans—yes, real, living, breathing fans! How cool is that? Most of our fans totally rock. Of course there are a few that are a little crazier than we were expecting.

Anyway, find out all about our funny fan encounters with these amazing photos and pages of, um, words. So microwave some popcorn (obviously not in a metal container!) and settle in to check it all out. Just don't eat too much because your stomach will hurt from all the laughing you're about to do. (Seriously—too much giggling plus too much food does not equal a good time.) Well, now I made myself hungry, so please turn the page so I can go eat. Catch you later!

;-)

Oh! And don't fo

w!

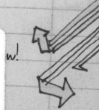

¡Am Your Biggest Fan!

Adapted by Laurie McElroy

Part 1: Based on "iNevel"
Written by Steve Holland

Part 2: Based on "iAm Your Biggest Fan,"
Written by Jake Farrow

Based on the TV series *iCarly*
Created by Dan Schneider

SIMON AND SCHUSTER

SIMON AND SCHUSTER
First published in Great Britain in 2010 by Simon & Schuster UK Ltd,
1st Floor, 222 Gray's Inn Road, London WC1X 8HB
A CBS Company

Originally published in the USA by Scholastic, 2010

A CIP catalogue record for this book is available from the British Library

ISBN 978-1-84738-796-7

10 9 8 7 6 5 4 3 2 1

Printed by CPI Cox & Wyman, Reading, Berkshire RG1 8EX

www.simonandschuster.co.uk and www.nick.co.uk

Part One

iNevel

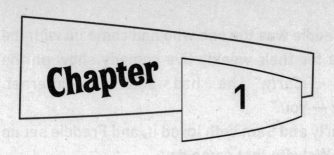

Chapter 1

Carly Shay and her best friend Sam Puckett decided to publicize their weekly Webcast in an unusual way. They decorated a supermarket cart with colorful signs that read "iCarly.com," and wheeled their technical producer, Freddie Benson, through the halls of Ridgeway School.

The halls were filled with kids at their lockers, stowing their coats, checking their homework, and getting ready for the first class of the day.

"Hey, watch *iCarly* this weekend," Carly said to a passing classmate.

"It's going to be hot," Sam added.

The plan was to tell everybody in school about their new Web show. Freddie had printed up a bunch of flyers to let kids know where and when they could find *iCarly* online. Freddie handed out flyers to anyone who would take them. "iCarly-dot-com," he said.

Freddie was the one who had come up with the name for their weekly live comedy show on the Web. "*iCarly*," he had said. "i — Internet. Carly — you."

Carly and Sam both loved it, and Freddie set up their Website that same day.

He had also volunteered to be the show's producer. It helped that he had all the latest camera equipment and knew how to use it. Plus, his apartment was right across the hall from the downtown Seattle loft Carly shared with her older brother, Spencer.

Sam — short for Samantha — was Carly's funny co-host on the show and her real life best friend. Sam was crazy, fun, and unpredictable on-screen and off. She was also a great friend. Carly couldn't do the show without her.

Carly only wished that Freddie and Sam wouldn't fight quite so much. She was always playing peacemaker and it got a little old after a while. Trying to keep Sam from doing Freddie bodily harm was almost a full-time job!

Carly had gotten the idea for the Webcast when the school refused to include kids with cool and

unusual talents in the annual Ridgeway talent show. She thought the world needed to see the pogo-hopping trumpet player, the kid who could say everything backwards, and especially the girl who could scratch her back with her feet! Who wouldn't crack up watching that?

The teachers, well, one in particular, Miss Briggs, at Ridgeway disagreed. She was more into "serious" and rather lame talents. So Carly created her own talent show on the Web — one that would allow kids to do and say what they want!

That first show had been such a blast that Carly and her friends decided to appear on computer screens all over the world every single week. Together Carly, Sam, and Freddie had come up with some great shows, but their audience wasn't as big as they'd like it to be. Not yet anyway. Spreading the word about iCarly.com at school was the first step in getting more viewers.

Carly spotted Wesley, a classmate who was obsessed with beatboxing, coming down the hall. As usual, he bopped around with a microphone in his hand, using his mouth and lips to create a drum beat.

"Hey, Wesley, watch *iCarly* this weekend," Carly told him. "It's going to be a great show."

Freddie handed Wesley a flyer. "iCarly-dot-com," Freddie reminded him.

Wesley took the flyer but didn't miss a note. He kept sputtering his beatbox tune into his microphone. He danced in front of them, blocking their way.

A little beatboxing was more than enough as far as Carly was concerned. "Okay, see ya," she said, giving him a nudge.

Wesley took the hint. He continued bopping on down the hall.

Sam handed their flyer to a girl from her history class. "Hey, check out our Web show at iCarly-dot-com," Sam said.

Another kid they had known forever was standing in the middle of the hall, digging through his backpack.

"Hey, Jeremy, you've heard of our Web show, right?" Carly asked.

"Sure. I've seen every episo —" Jeremy's answer was cut off when he sneezed loudly, followed by a cough and three more sneezes.

4

Carly and Sam jumped back to avoid the germs hurtling through the air.

Freddie was stuck in the cart and couldn't move. He tried not to breathe. "Flyer?" Freddie asked Jeremy.

"Yes, please." Jeremy took the flyer and blew his nose in it, coughing and sneezing a few more times. "Thank you," he said. He wiped his nose on the flyer again and tried to give it back to Freddie.

"You keep that," Freddie said.

"You're nice," Jeremy choked. Then he trudged off to the nurse's office to look for more tissues.

Carly watched him go and then realized that the last time she had talked to Jeremy he was wheezing and coughing just like he was today. The kid always seemed to have a stuffy nose. "Didn't he have a cold last week?" she asked.

Freddie nodded. "Last week. And the week before that."

"Why are we talking weeks?" Sam asked. "That lump's been blowing his nose nonstop since first grade."

It was true, Carly realized. Jeremy was a walking cold factory. In fact, she couldn't remember a

time when his nose wasn't bright red from sneezing.

Speaking of noses, Carly spotted a girl walking by who always had hers up in the air. "Hey, Tasha, check out our Web show this weekend," Carly said.

Tasha flipped her long, dark hair over her shoulder and took the flyer as if she was doing Carly a favor. Her friend Nicole stood behind her, ready to agree with anything that Tasha said.

Tasha had that effect on people, Carly noticed. Half of the girls at school followed her every move.

"iCarly-dot-com?" Tasha asked condescendingly.

"That's us," Carly said brightly.

"We rock," Sam added with a nod.

Tasha didn't agree. She looked at the flyer dismissively. "If your Web show was worth checking out, I'd have read about it on Nevelocity-dot-com," she said.

"Hey, just because our show wasn't reviewed on Nevelocity doesn't mean it's not cool," Sam said defensively.

Tasha rolled her eyes and shared a smirk with Nicole. "Actually, it does," she said. "Nevel writes about everything that's cool on the Web. And since he's never written anything about" — she stopped and looked at the flyer again — "*iCarly*, I guess your Web show's lame."

Tasha shrugged and turned her back on Carly, Sam, and Freddie, letting the flyer drop to the floor as if it was trash. She and Nicole strutted down the hall, convinced that Tasha had said the last word on the matter.

Carly and her friends watched Tasha go, seething with anger and frustration. For whatever reason, Tasha was one of the girls in school that other kids looked up to. If Tasha told the whole school that *iCarly* was lame, lots of kids would stop watching. And how many others were too polite to say that if Nevel didn't give *iCarly* a good review they wouldn't watch, either?

Tasha would enjoy nothing more than hearing that they gave up on their show because they had no viewers.

"She irks me," Carly muttered.

Sam narrowed her eyes. "I want to do bad things to that chick," she said.

Normally Freddie disagreed with whatever Sam had to say, but not this time. "You should." Freddie nodded.

Sam kept her eyes on Tasha's back, thinking about ways to get even with her for insulting their show. "I will," she said with a determined expression.

"Cool," Freddie said. "What are we gonna —"

Freddie stopped mid-question when Sam gave the supermarket cart a strong push. Suddenly, he was rolling down the hall after Tasha. The cart was completely out of control, and Freddie was trapped inside.

"Whoa! Whoa!" Freddie yelled. "What are you doing? I didn't mean me!" A lunch lady had to leap out of his path. Then he almost careened right into the math club. "Look out!" he shouted.

Kids jumped out of Freddie's way just in time, but now there was nothing between the cart and Tasha and it was gaining speed. The next thing Freddie knew, he had crashed right into Tasha

8

and her friends, and they all landed in a heap on the floor.

Carly and Sam cringed, viewing the carnage. Luckily, it didn't look like anyone got seriously hurt. They ran up the stairs to their first class before anyone could come looking for revenge.

That afternoon after school Carly sat in front of her computer reading the Nevelocity Website. If a review from Nevel would make people watch *iCarly*, then she would just have to ask him to check out the next episode. She knew he'd love it and write a fabulous review.

She was in the middle of her email to Nevel when her brother, Spencer, came home, loaded down with so many grocery bags that he could barely see over the tops of them.

Carly's father, a military officer, was stationed on a submarine. So her older brother, Spencer, was her guardian. Spencer was an artist. He was always creating sculptures out of cool stuff that no one else wanted. Carly never knew what she

would come home to next — a giant jack-o-lantern, a fan made out of hammers, a tree made out of magnets. Spencer was definitely creative, but he was also a great guardian. He made sure Carly ate right, went to school, and always had great advice. And Carly made sure Spencer didn't get too carried away with his wacky ideas. The two of them looked out for each other.

"Hey, kiddo, I'm home and I've got bags," Spencer said.

"Oh, yay, you went shopping," Carly said, getting up to help him. She had noticed that the cupboards and refrigerator were looking a little bare. Carly followed Spencer into the kitchen and opened one of the bags. "What'd you get?" she asked.

"Well, y'see . . ." Spencer started to explain.

Carly pulled package after package of the same item out of the grocery bag. "Butter . . . butter . . . butter," she recited. Then she pulled out another. "Oh, look. Butter," she said with a laugh. Were all the bags filled with butter?

"I bought a lot of butter," Spencer said seriously.

"Clearly," Carly replied. As much as she liked butter, she had hoped to find food, too. They needed milk. They needed eggs. They needed bread. They most definitely did not need any more butter. "This is all you got?" she asked.

"*Nooooo*," Spencer said. He pulled one more item from a bag. "I also got this thingy that makes the water in your toilet turn blue."

Carly laughed again. "Great, so for dinner we can have butter and blue toilet water."

Spencer shook his head. "This butter's not for eating," he explained. "I got hired to create a big sculpture."

Now the five-year-supply of butter was starting to make sense. "Made of butter?" Carly asked.

"Yeah, for the Bread Convention." Spencer held up a colorful cartoon picture of a piece of toast wearing a big white chef's hat and white gloves. The speech bubble over his head read, "GO TOAST!"

"See, it's Toasty the Baker. He's the mascot, and they hired me to make a giant sculpture of him out of butter," Spencer told her.

"*Ahhhh,*" Carly said, nodding. It looked like Spencer had bought enough butter for the entire city of Seattle, but he was actually going to need it all to create his statue.

"Ask me what I'm getting paid," Spencer demanded.

"Okay, what are —"

Spencer was too excited to wait for her to ask the whole question. "Money, baby!" he shouted. It didn't even matter how much — he was way excited to be getting any money at all. This sculpture was a big deal. He was totally psyched.

"Sweet!" Carly said.

Spencer gave her a fist bump. "Sweet like corn syrup!"

Carly laughed. "High fructose?" she asked.

"The highest!" Spencer clapped his hands, changing the subject. "Okay, so what are we doing for dinner? What's that little tween belly hungry for?" he asked, tickling his sister.

Carly laughed again. "Whatever," she said. Clearly it wasn't going to be anything that Spencer picked up at the store this afternoon. They would definitely be going out to dinner. "First just let me

finish this email." She headed back to the computer.

"Sure. Who are you writing?" Spencer asked. He carried the butter to the refrigerator. It was a good thing it was almost empty. He needed to keep the butter cold.

"This guy, Nevel, who runs a big Website." Carly said, typing.

"Nevelocity," Spencer said, nodding.

"Yeah. I'm trying to get him to check out our next Webcast and maybe write a review of it," Carly explained.

"Oooh, that'd be killer. Everybody reads Nevelocity," Spencer said.

"No kidding," Carly answered, thinking of Tasha and her friends. She'd love to see Tasha eat her words and admit that *iCarly* was cool.

She typed the words "please write back", and signed her name before clicking SEND. "There. All set," she said. "Let's hit it." She stood, ready to talk about dinner.

"Uh, well, yeah," Spencer said sheepishly. He picked up his only non-butter grocery store purchase. "But first I was kind of hoping . . ."

Carly knew her brother well enough to know exactly what he was kind of hoping for. He wanted to play with his new toy. "You want to go make the toilet water turn blue," she said.

"So much!" Spencer told her.

Carly laughed. "Do it."

Spencer grabbed the package and raced down the hall toward the bathroom. A few seconds later, Carly heard the toilet flush. The mission must have been a success, because she could hear Spencer cheering.

"Yeah!" Spencer yelled, running back into the living room.

"Happy?" Carly asked.

"Uh-huh," Spencer said with a smile.

Together, they left the apartment in search of dinner.

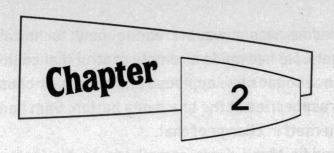

Chapter 2

The next night, Carly and her friends got ready for their weekly live Webcast. They all hoped that Nevel would watch and post a good review on his Website.

When they started doing their show, Carly, Sam, and Freddie had turned the third floor of Carly and Spencer's loft into their Web studio. It was a big, open space, and they had fixed it up to look totally amazing. There was plenty of room for all of Freddie's high-tech equipment, and Spencer's light sculptures made awesome props. He had also painted flames on the front end of a Mustang convertible, a classic car, which was in the background of every show. Behind it, they had painted a wall navy blue and added a moon and stars. A neon *iCarly* sign hung over the window, along with a LIVE sign that lit up when they were taping.

Freddie was always creating new technical gadgets. He had made a remote control that could produce sounds like applause and cheers, or boos and raspberries at the touch of a button. Sam had put herself in charge of that.

Freddie typed some commands on his laptop while the girls jumped around to get their energy up for the show. When everything was ready, Freddie picked up his handheld camera and began the countdown.

"In five . . . four . . . three . . . two. . . ." he said. Instead of saying the number one, he pointed at Carly and Sam and the red light on his camera blinked on. They were streaming live on the Web.

"Hey! Welcome to *iCarly*!" Carly said into the camera.

Sam smiled into the lens. "Check out our flashy new graphic."

Freddie clicked a button on his tech belt and a vibrating *iCarly* logo with pictures of Carly's and Sam's head pulsed across their viewers' computer screens. Music played in the background, and Carly and Sam made loud siren sounds.

The graphic disappeared and Carly and Sam stopped making their funny noises.

Carly smiled at the camera again. "Okay, I'm Carly . . ." she said.

Sam popped in front of her. As usual, they talked fast and finished each other's sentences. "I'm Sam."

"And we like to draw families on our toes!" Carly announced with a big smile.

"Observe!" Sam said.

The girls quickly lay down on their backs and kicked their legs up in the air so that their feet were right in front of Freddie's camera lens. He focused on their toes, which had cute little faces drawn on them. The girls did indeed have families on their toes!

Carly wiggled her toes.

Freddie pushed another button and a rumbling sound filled the studio. He shook the camera.

"Uh-oh," Carly said.

"Earthquake!" Sam yelled.

The girls jiggled their legs, screamed, and wiggled their toes at the camera, as if an

earthquake was throwing around their little feet families.

Freddie cracked up. It was exactly the kind of crazy and bizarre stunt that made the first few *iCarly* shows so funny. Some of their viewers had even started to send in videos of their own crazy comedy feats.

As soon as Carly and Sam finished with their earthquake bit, they aired one of the funnier viewer videos — a kid juggling Jell-O. Next up was a girl singing "The Star Spangled Banner" with teaspoons stuck to her face.

Carly and Sam burst out laughing, watching the video on the flat screen TV monitor in the studio.

"Okay, now if you thought that video was cool," Carly said into the camera.

"Check out this kid from New York," Sam said.

"He's a crump dancer," Carly explained.

Sam nodded seriously. "He enjoys crumping."

Then Carly got to the truly fun and crazy part that made it a perfect video for *iCarly*. "And he does it covered in peanut butter!"

"Crump it up, Peanut Boy!" Sam said.

Freddie typed in a command on his laptop, and the girls turned to the TV screen. A fourteen-year-old *iCarly* fan was covered in peanut butter from head to toe, and he was crumping!

"iCarly-dot-com," he said, coming to the end of his number.

Carly cracked up watching the peanut butter fly. "Unbelievable," she said.

"But is he smooth or crunchy?" Sam asked.

Carly had another question. "And does he have a girlfriend covered in jelly?"

Together the girls yelled into the camera, "Important questions!"

Sam used her remote to click off the monitor, and the TV screen automatically flattened against the wall — another one of Freddie's cool technical gadgets.

Carly turned to the camera. "Okay, next here on *iCarly* we're going to —" She was interrupted by the sound of the loft's elevator traveling to the third floor. She looked at the camera with a confused expression. "Who's coming up in the elevator?" she asked.

Sam looked embarrassed. "Oh . . . I . . . uh . . ."

The elevator doors opened with a ding. A delivery guy was standing there holding a box full of take-out containers. Freddie didn't know what else to do so he turned his camera on the delivery guy as he stepped out of the elevator. The smell of Kung Pao chicken and egg rolls drifted across the studio.

The guy stopped short when he saw the camera.

Carly and Sam smiled awkwardly at him while Freddie panned his camera from the girls to the delivery guy and back again.

Carly eyed Sam with a confused expression.

"I ordered Chinese food," Sam said sheepishly.

"During the show?" Carly asked, totally amazed.

Sam shrugged. "There's no wrong time to eat an egg roll," she said into the camera.

Carly thumped her friend on the forehead, and then turned back to her viewers. "Okay! It looks like we have a surprise visitor here on *iCarly.*"

She and Sam ran over and stood on either side of the delivery guy. His eyes darted from the girls to the camera and back again.

"Hi, Food Delivery Guy!" Sam said.

Carly gave him a huge smile. "What's your name?" she asked.

"Chuck," he answered, looking more and more confused and embarrassed.

Carly and Sam smiled into the camera and said his name together. "*Chuuuuuuuuck.*"

"Have you ever been interviewed, Chuck?" Carly asked.

Chuck smiled, but it looked more like a grimace. "No," he said flatly.

That didn't matter to Carly and Sam. Soon they had Chuck sitting in the middle of the studio with his box of take-out containers in his lap. They pulled up chairs on either side of him and tried to conduct an interview. Chuck wasn't the most brilliant conversationalist in the world, but it didn't matter how awkward and confused he was, Carly was going to make this work. She knew Nevel might be watching.

"So, Chuck, where are you from?" she asked.

"Wisconsin," Chuck said flatly. He stared down at the food in his lap.

Sam waited for him to say more, but Chuck was

clearly finished answering the question. She held up her remote and pressed the button for cheers and applause. The sound filled the studio while Chuck stared blankly at the camera.

"Are you in college?" Sam asked.

"No," Chuck answered.

"Okay," Carly said, grasping for something — anything — that would make this interview even a little bit interesting. A fantastic idea popped into her mind. "Oh! What's the weirdest thing that ever happened to you while you were delivering food?"

Chuck's face lit up for a minute, and Carly thought they might actually get an interesting story out of him. Then his face went blank again. Carly's heart sank when she realized that Chuck didn't have an answer.

"I don't know," Chuck said.

Sam waited a second, hoping that he would come up with a story. But Chuck had nothing to say, and Sam wasn't as polite as her friend was. "Chuck, you're very boring," she told him.

Carly realized they were going to have to save this situation somehow. "And that means it's time for this," she announced, jumping to her feet.

Sam knew what Carly was hinting at. She pressed a button on the remote and crazy lights started to flash. Dance music filled the studio, and a disco ball lowered from the ceiling.

When all else failed, it was time for crazy dancing! Carly and Sam started to jump around and dance like wild maniacs. Chuck sat there watching them until Carly and Sam pulled him to his feet. The food fell to the floor, forgotten, and soon Chuck was dancing, too. He danced like a tin man in serious need of an oilcan, but it was better than nothing.

Finally, they brought that week's episode of *iCarly* to an end. Carly could only hope that it was enough to get a good review from Nevel.

Chapter 3

As soon as they finished their Webcast, the *iCarly* team headed to the kitchen for drinks and Chinese food. Freddie and Sam were on the Website, checking for viewer responses, while Carly poured them lemonade.

Carly shook her head. "Our most important Webcast ever and you bring on a food delivery guy who was born without a personality," she said to Sam.

Sam was unapologetic. "The show was still awesome," she said.

Freddie clicked around on the *iCarly* Website. "Hey, you got an email from Nevel Papperman," he said to Carly.

Sam was totally psyched. "Nevelocity!" she yelled.

"Move!" Carly gasped and pushed Freddie out of his seat so that she could see the computer screen.

Freddie hit the floor with a thud.

Sam tried to read over Carly's shoulder. "C'mon! What'd the man say?"

"He says that he loved our Web show, and he wants to interview me," Carly said, her voice rising with excitement.

Sam couldn't believe it. "Oh my gosh!" she yelled.

"Yes!" Freddie said, pumping his fist in the air.

They all knew that if Nevel loved *iCarly* and was willing to write about it on his Website, their audience would skyrocket! And better yet, Tasha would have to admit that their show wasn't lame.

While the *iCarly* team was checking out Nevelocity, Chuck finally was able to prove that he had a personality. They heard the toilet flush, and the food delivery guy raced into the kitchen cupping water in his hands — blue toilet water!

"Hey! Your toilet water's blue! Lookit!" he yelled. He held his hands up to show them, but of course the water dripped to the floor. The palms of his hands were blue.

Chuck may have had a personality, but he didn't have a lot of smarts. "I'll get more!" he exclaimed, running back toward the bathroom.

Carly couldn't believe it. If Chuck had been that goofy on the show, it would have been hilarious. Where was this side of him when they needed it? "Now he gets a personality," she said sarcastically.

Spencer must have missed that part of the Webcast. He watched Chuck run down the hall and back to the bathroom waving his blue hands in the air. "Who's the dude playing in our toilet?" he asked.

Spencer was working on his butter sculpture when Carly came home from school the next day. She headed upstairs to get ready for her interview with Nevel while Spencer put the finishing touches on Toasty the Baker. He smoothed out the butter on Toasty's arm, and then stepped back to take in the big picture. He added a white chef's hat to the top of Toasty's head. The sculpture was perfect.

Carly came downstairs, ready to go. She noticed a distinct change in the air temperature when she hit the bottom step. "Hey. Why's it so cold in here?" she asked.

"Oh, I turned the air conditioner up so my butter sculpture won't melt," Spencer explained.

"Ah," Carly said. She hoped the Bread Convention would pick up the sculpture soon. She didn't want to have to live in an icebox. "So, are you ready to drive me to Nevel's for my interview?" she asked.

"Yep. Let's hit it." Spencer wiped his hands on a towel and tried to pick his car keys up off the counter, but they slipped right out of his hands. He tried again, and got the same results. "My hands have, um . . ."

"Butter," Carly said. Her brother was giving a whole new meaning to the phrase "butterfingers."

"Yeah," Spencer agreed, wiping his hands again. "I've got them though."

Only he didn't. Spencer tried a few more times to pick up his keys, and each time they slipped right out of his grasp. Finally, he picked them up with his teeth. "Let's go," he said from between clenched teeth.

Carly laughed. "Let's," she said.

A few minutes later, Carly and Spencer were at the address Nevel had given them in his email. They walked onto the house's front porch, and Carly rang the doorbell.

"I really think you should wait in the car," Carly said. She didn't think it looked very professional to have her big brother on hand for her interview.

"No way," Spencer told her. "You don't know this Nevel guy. What if he's a weirdo?" Spencer realized he was still wearing traces of his sculpture. "*Awww*, I got butter on my elbow." He tried to lick his elbow clean and couldn't reach it with his tongue.

The word "weirdo" was still reverberating in her mind while Carly watched Spencer twisting this way and that, trying — and failing — to lick his elbow. Didn't he know it couldn't be done? What if this Nevel Papperman guy saw Spencer and decided that she and her brothers were the weirdos? "Spence," she said.

"Uh-huh?" he mumbled, still trying to reach his elbow with his tongue.

"It's not possible!" Carly yelled.

Spencer stopped trying just in time. The front door opened and a woman greeted them with a friendly smile. "Hi, you must be Carly."

"Yes, ma'am, and this is my brother, Spencer," she answered.

"Nice to meet you," Spencer said.

"Please come in," the woman said, leading them into the living room. "Nevel is so excited to meet you. He's been talking about your Web show all week. He just loves it."

"Well, I'm a big fan of his Website," Carly said.

"Oh, thank you," Mrs. Papperman answered.

"How long have you and Nevel been married?" Spencer asked.

Mrs. Papperman turned to him with a surprised expression. "Married?" Then she started to laugh. "I'm sorry, I think you might be mistaking him for someone much —"

At that moment, Nevel walked into the room. Carly and Spencer realized why Mrs. Papperman

29

was laughing. Nevel wasn't her husband. He was her son!

Carly couldn't believe that the guy behind Nevelocity.com was a little kid. The guy who told people all over the country which Websites were cool and which ones were lame was actually younger than Carly and her friends. In fact, he looked like he was around eleven years old.

"Carly Shay, live and in person," Nevel said, walking over to her. "It is so exciting to meet you." He shook her hand. "I'm Nevel Papperman."

Now Carly was even more surprised. Nevel might have looked like he was eleven, but he sounded like a forty year old. He dressed like one, too — he was totally prepped out, and he didn't have a hair out of place. "Oh . . . you're Nevel?" she said.

Spencer was amazed, too. "You're just a little kid," he said to Nevel. Then he turned to Carly. "He's so cute."

Nevel glared at Spencer, stone-faced. Clearly he didn't like being called cute. "I created and now run one of the world's most visited Websites, which gets over five million page-views per day,"

he said firmly. "I'm not cute." He uttered the word "cute" as if it was something disgusting.

But Spencer knew cute when he saw it. And Nevel was cute. "Yeah, you are," he said. "I can tell because I want to mess up your hair." He reached out and starting mussing Nevel's hair. "Who's cute?" he asked.

Nevel gasped.

Spencer did it again. "Who's a cute Nevel?" he asked in a baby voice. "Who gets five million page-views? You *dooooo*!"

Carly was horrified. Spencer was going to guarantee her a bad review!

Nevel's face turned white and then red with rage. He was absolutely furious. "Mother . . ." he said.

Mrs. Papperman tried to distract Spencer. "Why don't you and I go in the kitchen? I'll make you some tea."

Spencer was easily distracted. "Will there be lemon?"

"Yes," Mrs. Papperman told him.

"All right then!" Spencer said.

Carly watched him go into the kitchen with

relief. Nevel might have been a kid, but he was a kid with power. And Spencer was making him mad. If the show was going to get a good review on Nevelocity.com, Carly had to keep this kid happy.

Nevel fixed his hair, took a few deep breaths to calm down, and turned to Carly with a smile. He gestured toward the couch. "Please. Sit," he said.

Carly nervously sat on the couch. Nevel sat next to her and picked up a plastic bottle from the coffee table. He squirted something onto his hands and then offered the bottle to Carly. "Hand sanitizer?" he asked.

"Uhhh. . . ." Carly didn't quite know what to say. Was Nevel trying to say she wasn't sanitary?

"Do you know that trillions of germs are living on your hand-skin right now?" Nevel asked.

"Really?" she asked.

Nevel nodded seriously.

Ugh, Carly thought. *Trillions!* She grabbed the hand sanitizer and rubbed it all over her palms and fingers. "Thanks," she said.

"Sure," Nevel answered, sitting back. "You know, I was really impressed with your Web show."

32

Carly relaxed a little bit. "Thank you so much. That really means a lot."

"I know," Nevel said, staring into her eyes.

Carly looked away. *Conceited much*? she thought.

"I think my readers will be very interested to learn more about you." He leaned in closer. "What type of shampoo do you use?"

Shampoo? Who cared what type of shampoo she used? "Huh?" Carly asked.

Nevel leaned even closer and ran his fingers through Carly's hair. He stuck his nose in and gave it a big sniff.

Carly leaned back to get away from him, totally disgusted.

Nevel sat back again with a satisfied smile. "Kiwi Salon with jasmine for normal to dry hair?" he asked.

Carly pretended to be impressed, but she was seriously creeped out. "Wow, you have an amazing nose," she said with a nervous chuckle.

"Yes," Nevel said, satisfied with the compliment.

"You must love flowers," Carly said, searching for a way to change the subject.

"I hate flowers," Nevel answered, rolling his eyes. "Bugs sit on them and make poo."

Carly could see that just the idea of bug poo was upsetting Nevel. "Okay," she said slowly. This kid was really strange.

Nevel reached behind him and grabbed a frame from the sofa table. "Look at this," he said, handing it to Carly. "It's an X-ray of my brain."

"Ah, interesting," Carly said. Was she supposed to say something nice about his brain? This was getting weirder and weirder.

"Big, isn't it?" Nevel asked smugly.

"Yeah. That's one beefy brain you've got there," Carly said with an awkward laugh.

"Thank you." Nevel took the picture and carefully placed it exactly where it had been. "Are you hungry?" he asked.

"No," Carly said. All his talk of germs and bug poo and big brains had ruined any appetite she might have had.

Nevel jumped up and ran toward the kitchen. "I'll fetch you a snack," he said.

Carly was completely confused. Hadn't she just said no? "But . . ." Carly called after him.

Nevel didn't hear her, or didn't care. He was already gone.

Worried, Carly pulled her cell phone out of her pocket and dialed Sam.

"Yeah?" Sam said, answering her cell.

"Sam! Where are you?" Carly whispered into her phone.

"Your house, watching TV," Sam said casually.

"Well you're not going to believe —" Carly suddenly realized what Sam had just said. "My house? How'd you get in?" she asked.

"I know where you and Spencer hide the key," Sam told her. "How's the interview going?"

"Weirdly. First of all, Nevel's not a man. He's a kid," Carly said.

"What? How old?" Sam asked.

"Like, eleven," Carly said. "And he's creepy."

"Well, be nice to him," Sam warned her. "You know how important this review is for our show. Millions of people read his site. Don't upset the kid."

"But what if he —"

Carly's question was cut off when Nevel came back into the living room with a snack tray. Carly quickly snapped her phone closed and turned to Nevel with a nervous smile. Sam was right. She couldn't upset the kid. It would be the death of *iCarly* if she did.

Back in the loft, Sam hung up her phone and rubbed her arms. "Man, why's it so cold in here?" she said to herself. She walked over to the thermostat, turned it up, and headed back to the sofa.

She didn't notice when Toasty the Baker started to melt. The noise of the TV blocked the steady *drip*, *drip*, *drip* of butter hitting the kitchen floor.

Chapter 4

While Spencer's butter sculpture was melting, Nevel was proudly showing Carly the snack he had prepared for her. The one she didn't want. "I brought you crackers and some of my mother's homemade tapenade," he said.

"Tapenade?" Carly asked. She had never heard of tapenade, and it looked like dark brown goop. It didn't exactly look appetizing, especially when she had just been thinking about bug poo.

"It's a spread made of olives, garlic, and capers," Nevel told her. "Try some."

"Yeah, I don't think tapenade is something I'd, you know —" Carly was about to say "care to try", but Nevel wouldn't take no for an answer. He shoved a cracker into her mouth. She had no choice but to chew or spit it out. She chewed.

Carly tried to hide just how irritated she was, and then she discovered that the tapenade was delicious. She loved it. "Oh my gosh, that's awesome!" she said.

"Isn't it?" Nevel agreed. He sat again and patted the couch cushion next to him. "Please, sit."

Carly sat, but she was still feeling awkward and confused. What was with the hair sniffing and the food? Why wasn't Nevel interviewing her about her Web show?

Then Nevel scooted closer to her on the couch. He was practically on top of her! Carly leaned away, but that only made Nevel lean in closer. He gazed at her and batted his eyelashes. "Do you think fireplaces are romantic?"

Romantic? "Um, yeah, I guess," Carly answered. Where was this going?

"You've guessed correctly." Nevel clicked a button on the laptop computer on the coffee table. The screen was filled with a picture of a roaring fire. He held his hands in front of the computer screen as if he was warming them.

Carly wondered if there was bug poo on real logs, too.

Nevel turned to her again with a satisfied smile. "Do you like music?" he asked.

"Um, yeah, sure," Carly said.

Nevel hit another button on his laptop and slow music filled the room. He swayed back and forth to the rhythm, watching Carly for a few seconds, and then he asked, "Would you like to dance?"

Carly was finding this all way too weird and creepy. "Dance?" she asked.

Nevel held out his germ-free hand.

Carly took it and stood. Nevel was going *way* too far. She pressed the spacebar on Nevel's laptop and both the music and the fake fire disappeared. "Look, I don't want to sound rude, but I really didn't come here to dance. Can't you just interview me about the Web show?"

Nevel looked at her for a moment with a dreamy smile and then leaned in and gave Carly a kiss on the cheek.

Carly jumped back, totally creeped out. "Nevel!" she yelled.

Nevel was obviously very pleased with himself. "I stole a kiss, upon your cheek, and now another kiss I seek," he crowed. He puckered his lips and leaned in to kiss her other cheek.

Carly was furious. He had brought her here with the promise of an interview when he had really planned a date the whole time! There was no way he would be kissing her again. "Seek some tapenade!" she yelled. She grabbed a big handful of the olive spread and pushed it into his face.

Nevel sputtered with rage.

Carly didn't care. She was going to get out of there as fast as she could. She grabbed her coat and ran for the front door. "Spencer!" she called.

Spencer came out of the kitchen holding a fancy cup and saucer. He held his pinkie out, just like in the etiquette books.

Nevel was too angry to even wipe his face. "You shouldn't have done that, Carly Shay! You'll rue this day," he shouted. "You'll rue it!"

Carly looked over at Spencer and then fled out the front door. She couldn't get away fast enough.

Nevel turned around and trained his glare on Spencer.

Spencer only noticed the tapenade all over Nevel's face. He didn't see the angry expression underneath it. "You've got a little —" he pointed at

40

his own cheek to try and let Nevel know that he needed a napkin.

"Spencer!" Carly yelled from the porch.

Spencer put down his fancy cup and saucer and fled with his sister.

Back at the loft, Carly was so angry she could hardly even speak. The more she thought about it, the madder she got. Sam and Freddie watched her fume, trying to find out exactly what had happened.

Freddie had only just heard about Nevel's age. "Nevel's only eleven?" he asked.

"Yes, now stop speaking," Sam told him. She turned to Carly. "Tell us what happened."

Carly paced back and forth, too angry to stand still. "Okay. I go there. Nevel sat next to me. He sniffed my hair, he showed me an X-ray of his brain, he tried to make me dance, and then he kissed me!" Carly told them.

"Whoa! He kissed you?" Now Freddie was mad, too. He'd had a crush on Carly for as long as he could remember, and *he* had never kissed her. He hated that someone else had. "That jerk!" he snapped.

"Yeah," Carly agreed. "He's a jerk."

"Tell us what happened *after* he kissed you," Sam said.

"I pushed tapenade in his face, then he got furious, and said I'd rue the day."

Spencer picked his laptop up off the coffee table. On the drive home, he and Carly had realized that neither of them knew what the word "rue" meant. Just how bad was Nevel's threat?

There was another word in that sentence that Sam didn't recognize. "What is tapenade?" she asked.

"A spread made of olives, garlic, and capers," Carly said.

"*Ewwww*," Sam said.

Freddie made a face. "Gross."

"It's actually really good," Carly told them. She knew it sounded disgusting, but it tasted delicious. "I can't explain it." She started pacing again.

"And what'd he mean, you'd rue the day?" Freddie asked.

Sam had the same question. "Yeah, what does 'rue' mean?"

Carly threw her hands up in the air. "No one knows!"

"I've got it right here," Spencer told them. He opened his laptop and read the definition off the computer screen. "Roux — a mixture of fat and flour used to make sauces and soups."

Sam's forehead wrinkled with confusion. "Nevel called you a fat flower?"

Carly knew that couldn't be right. Nevel had intended something much worse. Spencer had the wrong word. "Try spelling it differently," she suggested.

Spencer typed in the word using a different spelling. On his first try he had spelled the word r-o-u-x. Now he tried r-u-e. "Oh, okay here," he said. "Rue — to regret. To wish that something had never been done."

"Uh-oh," Sam said.

A feeling of dread settled in Freddie's stomach. "You know what this means?" he asked.

"Of course. He's going to make me regret shoving tapenade in his face by trashing *iCarly* on his

43

stupid Website," Carly said. She was still too upset to sit, or even to stand still. She paced back and forth in front of the computer.

"We're dead," Freddie said with a nod. No one would watch *iCarly* after reading a review that completely trashed the show.

Carly sighed, touching her face. "I'm going to go scrub his creepy lip residue off my cheek."

Spencer had surfed over to the Bread Convention Website after looking up the word "rue." He saw a picture of Toasty and congratulated himself for the perfect likeness he had created from butter. Then all of sudden he realized that something was wrong — very wrong. "Hey, why isn't it cold in here?" He jumped to his feet. "Toasty the Baker. Oh, no!" he yelled.

Spencer ran to the kitchen, followed by Sam and Freddie. His awesome butter sculpture, his perfect likeness of Toasty the Baker, was gone. There was just a pile of melted butter on the floor, along with a white chef's hat and two white gloves.

"Toasty!" Spencer screamed.

Sam looked at the floor and wrinkled her nose. "Gross. It's like a giant baby threw up."

Spencer dropped to his knees and picked up handfuls of melted butter. It dripped through his fingers. "*Whyyyyy*?" he moaned. "*Whyyyyy*?"

Sam realized what had happened. She wasn't about to take the blame, so she turned to her favorite scapegoat — Freddie. "I told you not to turn the heat up," she told him.

Freddie's eyes got wide. She was blaming him? He hadn't done it! "What? I never even —"

Sam held her hands up to cut him off. "It's too late for apologies."

Freddie sputtered. "But I didn't turn the —"

"It's okay!" Spencer yelled frantically, trying to convince himself that it really was okay. Then he took a deep breath said it again, more calmly. "It's okay." He stood and wiped his hands on a towel, thinking about what he needed to do to clean up the mess. "I just need to get a mop and a bucket." Then he realized what he really needed. He was going to have to make another butter sculpture — and fast! "And twenty-eight more pounds of butter!" he shouted.

Spencer hurried toward the door. There was no time to lose. He tried to turn the knob, but once again his hands were too slick. Finally he used his elbows, only to find Freddie's mother standing in the hall.

She narrowed her eyes at him suspiciously. "Spencer."

"Mrs. Benson," Spencer said with a nod. Then he called over his shoulder to Freddie. "Freddie, your mom's here!"

Sam and Freddie came out of the kitchen.

"I came over because I heard screaming," Mrs. Benson said. "Freddie, are you all right?"

Freddie cringed. His mother was always checking up on him, and it was *always* embarrassing. "Yes, Mom."

"He's fine," Spencer told her, "but I've really got to —"

Mrs. Benson cut him off. "You know he's allergic to fruit."

Sam seized at any opportunity to make fun of Freddie. "*Awww*, who's got a fruit problem?" Sam teased.

"Not me," Freddie insisted. "I am not allergic to fruit!"

46

"Well, what if you were?" Mrs. Benson asked. She pointed at Spencer. "He'd probably give you an orange and then your face would puff up."

Sam laughed and raised her hand. "I would love that."

Spencer didn't have time for Mrs. Benson and her overprotective worries today. He had to get to the grocery store. In fact, he'd probably have to go to five or six grocery stores to get all the butter he needed. "Look, I gave him no fruit. Now please, I'm out of butter —"

Mrs. Benson cut him off again. "False!" she yelled accusingly. "I saw you come home yesterday carrying grocery bags filled with butter."

"You spied on me?" Spencer asked.

"No, I just happened to be glancing through my peephole," Mrs. Benson claimed.

"Well, that butter's gone," Spencer said, moving past her. "And so am I."

Mrs. Benson was really suspicious now. She yelled after him, "What've you done with the butter?" Whatever it was, Mrs. Benson was convinced it couldn't be good. She turned to Freddie with a

concerned expression. "Freddie, I want you to take a bubble bath tonight."

Freddie cringed again while his mother hurried down the hall after Spencer. She was determined to get to the bottom of the butter mystery.

"I didn't give him any fruit!" Spencer yelled over his shoulder and then disappeared onto the elevator.

Freddie steeled himself for another one of Sam's insults.

Sam took everything in with a deadpan expression. Then she turned to Freddie. "Cool mom," she said.

A couple of hours later, the *iCarly* team was hanging out in the studio, waiting for Nevel's review to appear on his site. They knew it was coming, and they knew it would be terrible. The question was, how terrible?

Carly and Sam paced nervously while Freddie keyed in the Web address.

"Nevelocity-dot-com," he said, typing on his laptop.

"This is going to be bad," Carly said.

Sam was hopeful. "Maybe not."

"He said I'd rue the day, and I have a feeling the ruing's about to begin," Carly said.

"Just because he hates you personally doesn't mean he's going to give our show a bad review," Sam insisted.

But Freddie had found the Website and the review. It wasn't good. "Get ready to rue," he warned them.

Carly and Sam ran over. "You found Nevel's review?" Carly asked.

"Read it!" Sam urged.

"*iCarly*," Freddie read. "Or, as it should be called, *iBoring* . . ."

"You see?" Carly said to Sam.

"Boring!" Sam exclaimed. You could call their show a lot of things, but boring wasn't one of them. It was wacky. It was exciting.

Carly steeled herself for the worst. "Keep going. Let's hear it."

"This Webcast stars Carly Shay, an unappealing thirteen-year-old girl," Freddie read.

Carly's eyes flashed with anger. She started to

yell at the computer. "Yeah, if I'm so unappealing, then why were you sniffing my hair and chomping on my cheek?"

"Keep going," Sam said.

Freddie read the rest of the review. "My advice: If you're trying to decide between watching *iCarly* or going to prison, choose prison. You'll have more fun in jail than you ever will at iCarly-dot-lame."

Dot-lame? Carly let out a disgusted sigh. "That is so unfair."

Freddie tried to find something positive to say to make Carly feel better. "At least he didn't call you a fat flower."

Sam remembered what Tasha had said in school. Everybody relied on Nevel's Website to clue them into what was cool and what was lame. And he had just said they were boring and lame. "Yeah, but now everybody's going to read that review and stop watching us," she said.

Carly thought about that for a minute. Her downcast face suddenly brightened when she got an idea. "No, they're not," she said.

"Why aren't they?" Freddie asked.

"Because we're going to make Nevel admit that he loves our Webcast and that he only wrote that mean stuff because I didn't want to be his little girlfriend," Carly said.

"Yeah," Sam agreed with a smile. She loved revenge. "Let's make him regret writing that review."

"Oh, he's not just going to regret it," Carly said happily. "He's going to *rue* it."

The next day, Spencer was still working on his second butter sculpture of Toasty the Baker. He was about halfway done when he stepped back to survey his work. He had finished Toasty's platform and his feet, and now he was building his buttery body.

"Don't worry, Toasty," Spencer said. "Soon you'll be back and butter than ever." He laughed at his own joke, and then realized how bad it was. "Thank goodness no one heard that," he said to himself.

There was a knock at the door.

"I'm coming," Spencer called, running over. He reached to turn the knob, and then remembered that his hands were covered in butter. He awkwardly opened the door with his elbows to find Nevel standing in the hall.

"I am Nevel," the eleven-year-old said. "I'm coming in now."

"Okay," Spencer said.

Nevel walked past Spencer and looked around with a sneer. "Carly invited me here," he said.

"I know," Spencer told him.

"She said she wants to apologize to me for her obnoxious behavior," Nevel said.

"Well, I think she feels bad about it," Spencer told him.

Nevel puffed up in a self-important way. "Good," he said. "Where is Carly?"

"Up on the third floor." Spencer pointed to show Nevel the way. "You can take the elevator or the stairs there."

Nevel spotted the half-finished sculpture. "What is that?" he demanded.

"Oh, I'm an artist," Spencer said, always happy to discuss his work. "I'm making a sculpture . . . out of butter."

Nevel sneered again. "Your work disgusts me," he announced dismissively. He turned on his heel and walked up the stairs.

Spencer watched him go, crumpling a little bit under Nevel's harsh criticism. "Nevel's a stupid name," he said under his breath.

Upstairs, Nevel opened the door to the studio expecting to find Carly. He had decided that if her apology was nice enough and humble enough, he might even change his review. But instead of finding Carly, he found an empty room.

"Carly? Hello?" He looked around. "Carly?"

Suddenly, out of nowhere, Carly's friend Jeremy grabbed Nevel from behind in a bear hug.

"What the —" Nevel shouted, struggling to break out of Jeremy's grasp. "Who are you? What's going on?"

Jeremy didn't answer. He was too busy coughing and sneezing — all over Nevel.

Carly, Sam, and Freddie entered the room. Carly was convinced that Jeremy the germ factory was the perfect tool to get Nevel to admit that he had lied about *iCarly*.

"Hello, Nevel," Carly said. "I see you've met our friend Jeremy."

Freddie smirked and crossed his arms over his chest. "Or as we like to call him, Germy."

Sam threw her arm around Carly and grinned. "The germiest kid in our whole school," she told Nevel.

"It's true," Jeremy said, holding on tight so Nevel couldn't escape. He coughed and sneezed at the same time to prove his point. "I'm a mess." He sneezed again, followed by a hacking cough.

Nevel turned his head and tried not to breathe. Germs were flying through the air all around him. Landing on his face! Germy hands were touching him. This was his worst nightmare. "Stop it!" he yelled trying to tear Jeremy's hands apart. "I can't stand germs."

"Then you'd better tell the truth," Sam said.

Carly walked in front of Nevel and put her hands on her hips. "Admit that you like *iCarly*."

"And that your review was a lie," Sam added.

Nevel was still struggling to get out of Jeremy's grasp. "Let go of me!" he yelled.

"Freddie, roll camera," Carly said.

Freddie picked up his camera, turned it on, and focused on Nevel. "Rolling," he said.

"Tell the truth, Nevel," Carly demanded.

"I don't know what you're talking about!" Nevel said through clenched teeth.

Jeremy coughed and sneezed some more.

Nevel fought to get free. "Stop it, sicko!" he yelled. "Let go of me!"

"No way," Jeremy said. "They're paying me to do this."

"How much?" Nevel demanded.

"Five bucks," Jeremy said.

Nevel offered Germy Jeremy a new deal. "I'll give you ten to release me."

That made a lot of sense to Jeremy. He had to buy a lot of tissues and cold medicine, and that cost money. "Deal," he said, letting go of Nevel.

Nevel turned on him. "Ha!" he yelled. "Now you get nothing." He spun on his heel and faced Carly. "You feel the rue? You feel it?" he demanded. Then he ran out of the room.

Nevel cackled happily as he dashed down the stairs and through the front door. He raced for the elevator, pausing only long enough to slather his hands and face with hand sanitizer.

Jeremy coughed apologetically. "He out-smarted me," he admitted.

56

"He outsmarted all of us," Freddie said.

Carly stamped her foot in frustration. "Why does he have to have such a big brain?" she asked.

Sam shook her head with a sigh. "So what are we going to do now?" she asked. She didn't have to remind her friends that as long as Nevel's negative review was posted on Nevelocity.com, people would think their show was lame and boring.

"I don't know," Carly said with a sigh. "How do you take down a brilliant, powerful eleven-year-old boy?"

Sam and Freddie looked at each other and shrugged. They were out of ideas. But then a slow smile spread across Carly's face. She had another inspiration, and this one would *have* to work!

By the next day, Carly's new plan was in place, and Sam and Freddie were ready to help. They decided to hit Nevel with it as soon as he came home from school.

"Mother, I'm home from school," Nevel said, coming through his front door and setting down his backpack. When he straightened up, he found Carly, Sam, and Freddie in the living room with his mother, and he recognized the look on his mother's face. She was angry. Very, very angry.

"Nevel Papperman. Did you write a bad review of this girl's Web show just because you were angry with her?" Mrs. Papperman demanded.

Nevel turned to Carly. "You told my mom on me?" he asked.

Carly nodded with a smile.

The fact that Nevel was avoiding her question didn't escape Mrs. Papperman. "Nevel!" she said.

"Okay, yes!" he admitted. "But only because she rubbed my face with tapenade!"

Carly wasn't about to let him get away with blaming that on her. "Because you kissed me in a surprise attack!" she insisted.

"*Shhh! Shhh!*" Nevel said. He really didn't want his mother to know about that.

Now Mrs. Papperman was even more surprised. "You told me you thought girls were yucky," she said.

Nevel cringed with embarrassment. He couldn't believe his mother had said that in front of the girl

58

iNevel

iAm Your Biggest Fan

he had a crush on. "That was last year!" he yelled. "I'm going through changes."

"You just go to your room and write an honest review of Carly's Web show," Mrs. Papperman told him, pointing to the stairs.

"Which you said you loved," Carly reminded him.

"A lot," Sam added.

Freddie glared at him. He was still angry about the stolen kiss. "Yeah, Papperman."

Nevel still didn't move. He glared at Carly and her friends.

His mother was firm. "Go on," she said, pointing to the stairs again.

Defeated, Nevel hung his head and trudged toward his room, stopping in front of Carly. "Can I call you?" he asked.

Carly couldn't believe it. After what he had done to her, this obnoxious germ freak still wanted to call her? "Get out of here!" she yelled.

Nevel moped his way out of the room, pausing to shoot a dirty look at Sam and Freddie. They coughed and sneezed on him.

Nevel ran for the stairs. "Germs!" he yelled.

Everyone watched him go, and then Mrs. Papperman decided to offer her guests a snack. "Tapenade?" she asked.

Carly was excited. The one good thing that had come out of all this Nevel nonsense was getting to taste Mrs. Papperman's tapenade and learning that she absolutely loved it. "Oooh, yeah!" she said. "And those little crackers."

Mrs. Papperman grinned and headed for the kitchen.

The *iCarly* team followed her, happy that Nevel's true review of *iCarly* would bring them more and more viewers. Never again could Tasha and her friends claim that *iCarly* must be lame because Nevel hadn't reviewed it. Plus they got awesome snacks!

Part Two

iAm Your Biggest Fan

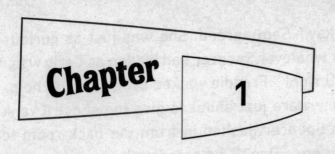
Carly let herself, Sam, and Freddie into the loft one afternoon after school for an *iCarly* planning session. They dropped their backpacks on the floor and were heading to the kitchen for a snack when they noticed something huge in the middle of the living room. There was a sheet draped over it.

"What is that?" Carly asked.

"Looks like a big sheet," Freddie said.

Obviously! Carly and Sam both gave Freddie looks that said "duh."

"I want to know what's *under* the sheet," Carly said pointedly.

Sam turned to Freddie. "And I want to know what's between your ears because it sure ain't brain," she said sarcastically.

Carly walked over to the object. There was only one way to find out what Spencer had covered up. "Help me pull this sheet off," she said.

"Okay," Sam agreed. She was just as curious about whatever Spencer had hidden as Carly was.

"All right." Freddie walked over, ready to help.

They were just about to give the sheet a yank when Spencer dashed in from the back room to stop them. "Don't!" he screamed.

Carly yelped and jumped back. Freddie froze on the spot. Even Sam grabbed her heart.

"Did I startle you?" Spencer asked more quietly, realizing that his scream had been a little over the top.

"Yeah," Carly told him.

"You did," Freddie agreed.

"Sorry," Spencer said. "But what's under that sheet is a big surprise, to make up for your last birthday."

Freddie remembered Carly's last birthday, and he didn't think there was anything to make up for. "I thought you bought her a lava lamp," Freddie said.

Carly shook her head. "He *made* me a lava lamp," she told him. "Which exploded."

Spencer corrected her. "It didn't explode. It burst into flames."

"And then exploded," Carly insisted.

"Well . . . yeah," Spencer admitted sheepishly. Then he quickly changed the subject. "Anyway, you know how you've been asking me to make you a cool, new sculpture for the *iCarly* studio?" he asked.

"Yeah. . . ." Carly said slowly. The memory of the exploding lava lamp had suddenly cooled her desire for a new piece of Spencer's art. Who knew what could happen?

"And you know the old car you guys got up there?" Spencer continued.

"Sure," Carly said.

Spencer thought he had said enough to grab their attention, and now he was ready for the big reveal. "Back up!" he said dramatically.

The *iCarly* team stood back while Spencer grabbed the sheet and yanked it off his sculpture with a dramatic flourish. Underneath was a vintage car seat to go along with the vintage Mustang convertible in the studio upstairs. The seat was upholstered in red leather. Spencer had also attached red and blue police lights to the back on either side.

"Oh my gosh!" Carly squealed.

Freddie couldn't believe how cool it was. "Look at that!"

Sam was totally speechless — a remarkable event all by itself.

Carly knew her brother was a talented artist, but even she couldn't believe Spencer had created something so perfect for the studio. "You made this?" she asked

"Heck yeah," Spencer said proudly. "I went to the junkyard — I have an account there — I found an old bench seat from a '66 Ford, reupholstered it, added cupholders, and installed real police lights." He ran he hands over the red leather, and pointed to the seat's various accessories.

Spencer was enjoying his sister's and her friends' reactions. It was clear they absolutely loved his newest creation. "It's art you can sit upon," he said dramatically.

"May we sit upon it?" Freddie asked.

"I'd be sad if you didn't," Spencer told him.

"Awesome," Sam said. She walked over and took a seat in the middle

"Let us sit," Freddie pronounced, dropping next to her.

It was the perfect size for the three of them.

Carly sat on Sam's other side. "Cool!" Only then did she realize that the bench seat wasn't just beautiful, it was comfy, too. "*Niiiice*," she said.

"Excellent," Freddie agreed.

Spencer couldn't wait to show them what else the seat could do. Those police lights weren't just decoration. "Wait, wait, let me turn it on." He flipped a switch and the police lights started to twirl. A siren wailed, sounding just like a real one.

"Whoa," Sam said. All kinds of fun ideas for the Webcast started to come to her. There was a lot they could do with those lights.

Carly watched the red and blue lights flash. "Sweet!"

Spencer pointed to a control panel attached to Carly's cupholder. "Now, push that button and you'll hear a real car horn."

"Okay." Carly pressed the button and listened to the sound of a horn honking. Unfortunately, at the same time, she also heard a small popping sound, and then a louder one. It was an explosion. She turned to watch flames erupt from one of the police lights.

All three kids jumped away from the seat and stared at the fire.

"Electrical wiring just isn't your thing," Carly told her brother.

Spencer stared at the flame with a frown. "No, it is not," he said. He sighed and reached for the fire extinguisher. He always had one at the ready. After all, you never knew where the next explosion was going to come from.

Later that afternoon, Carly and Sam headed up to the studio to talk about their upcoming Webcast. They were lying on their backs on beanbag chairs while they looked through colored index cards with ideas for the show.

"Okay. Sam gives Carly a haircut," Carly said, reading one. She looked over at Sam. Did the girl really think Carly would say yes to that? "What, are you serious?" she asked.

"I think our viewers would get a kick out of seeing me cut your hair," Sam said.

Carly shot her an "are you crazy?" look. "I'm not letting you near my neck with a pair of scissors."

"Fine, what else we got?" Sam said with a shrug.

The girls flipped through their index cards looking for something fresh and funny. Freddie came into the room sipping a glass of iced tea.

"Hey. What're you guys doing?" he asked.

"Looking through our show idea cards," Carly told him.

"We need one more fun thing to do on next week's *iCarly*," Sam explained.

Carly remembered something Freddie was working on. "Hey, did you ever get the software set up to do Twister-Vision?" she asked him.

Freddie walked over to his tech center. "Yeah, I think so, let me check." He opened his laptop and typed in some commands. "Yep, set to go," he said.

Problem solved.

"Good, we'll do Twister-Vision," Sam said.

"Yay!" Carly yelled. That week's show was fully planned. They could relax and have fun now.

"Woo-hoo." Sam squeezed her index cards together so that they flew up into the air and scattered.

Carly did the same.

"Hey," Freddie said, looking at his computer screen. "Listen to this comment one of our viewers wrote."

Sam had heard a few too many comments after last week's show. "If it's about that zit I had last week I don't want to hear about it."

"It was barely noticeable," Carly said, trying to be helpful.

"It was a volcano," Sam pronounced.

"Listen," Freddie said, reading the comment. "'My name is Mandy and I think *iCarly* is the awesome-est Web show on the whole Internet. I live near Seattle and I was wondering if you guys ever thought about having a live audience, because I'd love to come see the show in person. Please write back. Love and hugs — Mandy.'"

Freddie looked up. "And then she types the super-smiley emoticon like this" — he demonstrated a big, goofy grin for Carly and Sam.

Carly thought about it for a minute. "Live audience," she said to Sam. "What'cha think?"

Sam looked around the studio. It was big enough for the three of them, but there was no

place to put more than a couple of extra people. "We don't have room in here for an audience."

"We got Spencer's cool car seat he gave us," Carly pointed out. She walked over to the Mustang. Spencer had already carried the new seat upstairs — minus the exploding police lights.

"Yeah, I guess Mandy could sit there," Sam agreed.

"An audience of one?" Freddie asked.

"Why not?" Carly said.

"Let's do it," Freddie said with a shrug.

"I don't care," Sam added.

Carly spotted an index card she hadn't seen before and picked it up off the floor. Disbelievingly, she read it out loud. "Carly and Sam roll Freddie in bread crumbs then bake him at three-fifty!"

Freddie's jaw dropped. He glared at Sam. She was always coming up with ways to torment him, but this was over the top even for her.

"Just until he's golden brown," Sam said defensively.

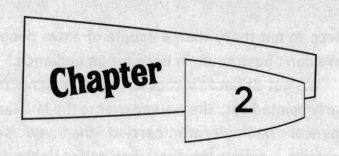

Chapter 2

The next night, Carly and Sam were in the middle of another awesome *iCarly* Webcast. Freddie, of course, was on hand to shoot all the action. Things were going well. So far the show had been really cool.

Sam got ready to introduce the next sketch. "Okay! Now it's time for a new segment on *iCarly* which we call..." She pressed a button on her remote and cheers and applause filled the studio.

Carly and Sam announced the title together for the camera. "'Twister-Vision!'"

Freddie keyed in a command and a colorful Twister-Vision graphic appeared on the screen, twisting and turning.

"It's the twistiest!" Carly said with a laugh.

Sam played the part of the consumer in a bad television infomercial. She turned to

Carly and asked robotically, "But how does it work?"

"Well, with the help of our technical producer, Freddie . . ." Carly said.

"That silly dude right there . . ." Sam added.

Freddie rolled his eyes, but kept his camera trained on the girls.

"We can alter reality," Carly finished.

Carly and Sam leaned into the camera, waving their hands and moving their bodies up and down. "Alter, alter, alter," they said, doing their best to make their voices sound ghostlike and spooky. "Alter, alter, alter."

"Okay, Freddie, start twisting this vision!" Sam said.

Freddie worked the controls on his technical panel. "Twisting the vision," he announced.

The live images of Carly and Sam started to morph and twist into weird shapes. The girls leaned into to each other so that they were cheek to cheek for the camera.

"*Wooo-aaaahhh . . .*" Carly said. Her face twisted back and forth as if she was standing in front of a funhouse mirror.

"*Bwaaaahhh...*" Sam said menacingly. Her faced stretched and bent into a bizarre, otherworldly picture.

"I'm *Carleeeeeee...*" Carly said, stretching out her name. Her face stretched, too, first in one direction, then the other. Her mouth looked incredibly wide.

"I'm *Saaaaaaaammmmm...*" her friend said, rolling her eyes and letting her face roll and morph for the camera. One second she was all nose. The next, her left eye was huge and her right one practically disappeared.

"She's *Saaaaaammmmm...*" Carly said.

"That was *Carleeeeee...*" Sam said.

"We're *giiiirrrrllllllzzzz...*" Carly said, knowing that they didn't really look like girls at the moment. They looked more like aliens.

Sam was getting really silly now, enjoying the way her mouth twisted and turned as she talked. "We have *haaaaiiiirr...*"

The girls started playing with their hair while they cackled for the camera. Their heads got bigger and smaller and then bigger again.

"*Bweeeeeeeeeee!*" Carly shouted.

74

"*Mwaaahahahahaa!*" Sam drawled.

They got a look at themselves on the monitor and cracked up.

"Okay, Freddie. Back to reality," Carly told him.

Freddie spun himself around and typed in the command. "Restoring reality," he said, and the video returned to normal.

Carly laughed again. "Okay, now we're going to throw something else new at you."

Sam looked into the camera and started to explain. "The other day, we were checking the comments here at iCarly-dot-com . . ."

". . . and we found a girl who's got to be the biggest fan of this Web show ever," Carly finished.

"This chick's cuckoo for *iCarly*," Sam said. "So let's bring her out . . ."

Together, Carly and Sam announced their fan girl's name. "Mandy Valdez!"

Twelve-year-old Mandy ran into the studio. She ran right up to the camera. Her face filled the screen as she waved excitedly to the viewers at home. "Hi! Hey, everyone! Hello! I'm on *iCarly*. Heh. Heh." Everything she said was punctuated by nervous, little laughs.

Mandy was so excited she was jumping up and down, and she couldn't seem to stop saying hello. "Hey. Hi. Hello," she babbled. "Heh. Heh."

Freddie pulled back so that Carly and Sam were back in the shot. Mandy stood between them.

"How are you doing, Mandy?" Carly asked.

"Welcome to the show," Sam said.

Mandy laughed again. "Heh. Heh. I made cookies for you guys. Lookit." She held up a tray for Carly and Sam.

"*Awwwwww,*" Carly said, picking up her cookie.

"That's so nice," Sam said, looking at hers.

Both girls were surprised to see that Mandy had decorated the cookies to look exactly like them. Carly's had dark brown hair and big brown eyes. The cookie even wore a pink heart necklace like the one Carly often wore. Sam's cookie had wavy blond hair and a big smile.

"Wow," Carly said.

Sam showed hers to the camera. "She put our faces on the cookies."

"Freddie, zoom in on this," Carly requested.

The girls held their cookies up, and Freddie zoomed in. Carly and Sam moved the cookies as if they were talking.

"I'm Carly," Carly said in a high voice.

"I'm Sam," Sam said, speaking for her cookie. "My face is delicious."

"There's a chocolate chip in my brain," Carly joked. "*Weeee*!"

"*Woooo*!" Sam's cookie responded.

Mandy giggled. "You guys made my cookies talk. That is so funny." She pulled Carly into a tight hug.

Mandy's reaction was a little too extreme, Carly thought. She didn't quite know what to say.

"Yeah, well . . ."

Mandy jumped in. "Ooo! I made a Freddie cookie, too." She ran up to the camera, getting way too close. Her face filled the lens again. "Here's your cookie, Freddie."

"Thanks," Freddie said, taking it from her.

Mandy's face was still planted right in front of his camera, and Freddie couldn't back up any further.

"Um, you're a little close to the lens," he told her. He didn't think the *iCarly* viewers wanted

such a tight close-up of the show's number one fan.

"Oops. Heh. Heh." Mandy stepped back with a nervous little laugh. She looked around, wondering what was next.

"Mandy, since you're *iCarly*'s first live audience member ever . . ." Carly told her.

"Please step this way," Sam continued. "Where you'll be able to watch the show while sitting upon what we call the . . ."

Carly and Sam looked into the camera and announced together, "*Seat of Sitting*!"

A graphic of the red leather bench seat popped up on the screen.

"*Ooooo*," Carly and Sam said together.

"Okay!" Mandy ran over to seat and plopped herself down right in the middle. She stared at Carly and Sam, waiting for the next fun thing to happen.

Carly realized she should tell their viewers more about the cool bench. "And I should point out that this amazing seat was made by my brother —"

Mandy cut her off with a yell. "Spencer!" she shouted, giggling. "That's your brother's name. Heh. Heh."

"Wow, this girl really knows her *iCarly*," Sam said, realizing just how hard it was going to be to do the show if Mandy kept interrupting.

Carly realized the same thing. "Yes, she does," she said awkwardly.

Mandy didn't pick up on their discomfort. "It's true, I do." She giggled again. "This seat is comfortable." She bounced up and down on it for a minute and then settled down. She stared at Carly and Sam with an expression that said, "hurry up and be funny."

"Go on, do your thing," she ordered with a giggle.

Now it was Carly and Sam's turn to chuckle nervously. They looked at each other and then into the camera, their smiles fading into worried frowns. Had they made a huge mistake in inviting Mandy to the show? Would their viewers keep watching if she kept interrupting?

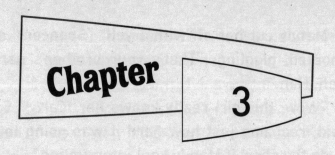

As soon as the show was over, Carly, Sam, and Freddie led Mandy down the stairs and toward the front door. They couldn't wait to get away from their number one fan and her nervous giggle. But Mandy was still bouncing up and down with excitement, and she couldn't seem to stop talking about how much she loved everything she saw.

"These stairs are awesome," Mandy babbled. She looked around at the living room and kitchen. "So this is the first floor of your guys' apartment? Heh. Heh. This is like where you eat meals and socialize?"

"Uh-huh," Carly said.

"Cool!" Mandy said, looking around again. She spotted an old, ratty drum set in the middle of the floor. "Who plays the drums?" she asked, running over to them.

Carly shrugged. The drums hadn't been there when she went upstairs to start the show. "I don't know. I'm not sure why those are here."

Mandy giggled. "Oh. A mystery!"

Sam rolled her eyes. She was tired of being polite. Mandy had to go — now! "Yeah, well, I guess it's time for you to go," she said.

Freddie pointed to the door, hoping Mandy would walk through it and disappear out of their lives forever.

"Thanks so much for being our first live audience member," Carly said weakly. She didn't add, "and our *last* live audience member," but that's exactly what Carly was thinking.

"Thank me? Are you kidding? Try thank YOU," Mandy insisted.

Spencer walked into the room. "Anybody seen my bottle of lotion?" he asked.

Mandy started jumping up and down with excitement again. She recognized Carly's older brother from the appearances he had made on the Webcast. "Spencer!" she screamed, rushing to him. "How are you?" She wrapped her arms around him and gave him a big hug.

Spencer was totally confused. He had no idea who Mandy was, but she certainly seemed to know him. She was looking up at him with a big smile.

"Great, awesome," Spencer said awkwardly. He searched his memory for some clue as to who was hugging him, and came up blank. "Wow, I haven't seen you . . . since . . . the past." He looked over Mandy's head to Carly and her friends for help.

Freddie rolled his eyes. "That's Mandy."

Spencer was still confused.

"She watches our show a lot, so we had her on as a guest tonight," Carly explained.

"You don't know her," Sam added.

Spencer unwrapped Mandy's arms from around his waist and took a step back. If he didn't know her, what was with the big hug?

But Mandy simply ran in and hugged him again. This time Spencer moved her away more force-fully and steeled himself to push her away again.

Mandy stayed put, but she seemed to be hover-ing on the edge of throwing herself at him again. Spencer ran over and stood behind the drum set so that she couldn't get her hands on him.

"Hey, what's up with the drums?" Carly asked.

"Yeah, we were curious," Mandy said with a giggle.

"Right. Well, um, there was a flyer in the lobby for a band that needs a drummer," Spencer explained. "So, I found these at the junkyard, and I'm going to fix them up and try out."

The junkyard? Carly wondered just how good the drums could be if someone else had thrown them away, but it wouldn't be the first time Spencer had turned someone else's junk into his treasure.

"Awesome!" Mandy shouted.

Spencer headed for the kitchen to get away from her.

"Well, all right, Mandy, it was really nice meeting you," Carly said, trying to get rid of the girl.

"Yeah," Sam said, more than ready to say goodbye to Mandy forever.

Mandy didn't seem to get the hint that they wanted her to leave, or she didn't care. "What are you guys going to do now?" she demanded.

"Uh, we're just going to go across the street . . ." Carly said.

"Get some smoothies," Sam told her.

"Cool, let's do it," Mandy said. "I have money," she added quickly, before they could say no.

"Oh. You want to come with us?" Carly asked.

As far as Sam was concerned, Carly was being way too polite. "*Uhhhhhh* . . . Freddie, talk to Mandy," Sam said. She pushed Mandy over to Freddie and pulled Carly aside.

Freddie smiled at Mandy. He couldn't wait to get rid of her either. What was he supposed to talk to her about? "Hello," he said awkwardly.

Mandy stood much too close to him and smiled up into his face. "I like your camera work," she said. "Sweet zooms."

"Thank you. I do try my best to zoom sweetly," Freddie said.

Mandy giggled nervously.

Across the room, Sam was trying to talk Carly into telling Mandy she couldn't join them for smoothies. "Look, it already bums me out that Freddie comes with us. Now we've got to take her, too?" she asked. "You know how much I hate people."

Carly didn't have the heart to be mean to Mandy. "C'mon, she's our biggest fan and she wants

to buy us smoothies," she said. "What's the big deal?"

Sam sighed and looked across the room. She could tell she wasn't going to win this argument. Even if Carly suddenly agreed to be mean, Mandy wouldn't give up. "C'mon, Mandy, let's go to Groovy Smoothies," Sam said reluctantly.

"Awesome!" Mandy shouted. She ran to the front door. "We'll be like the Three Musketeers," she said happily.

Freddie looked around and did the math. "But there's four of us."

"Touché!" Mandy said, pointing at him. She turned and led the way to the elevator.

Mandy was totally oblivious to the fact that they didn't want to spend time with her. She was still just babbling on about berries. "What are your guys' favorite berries? I like cranberries, boysenberries, blueberries, blackberries, huckleberries; I also like Halle Berry. Heh. Heh."

Carly, Sam, and Freddie followed behind her, dragging their feet.

☺ ☺ ☺ ☺ ☺

Spencer worked on his junkyard drum set while Carly and her friends were at the Groovy Smoothie. He cleaned it up, shined it up, and put it all together. He tightened the last screw with satisfaction. He was ready to rock.

"There we go," he said to himself. "Let's see now." He picked up his drumsticks and hit the bass drum, and then the snare. The snare drum fell to the floor. Spencer looked at it, and then realized what the problem was. "I rocked too hard," he said to himself, shaking his head. *That band had better get ready for one powerful drummer*, he thought. When he auditioned, he would blow them away.

He was picking up the drum when Sam and Carly breezed through the front door with their smoothies.

"I just think that for five bucks they could blend it a little better," Sam was saying. "So I don't get strawberry lumps stuck in my straw."

Carly spotted Spencer at his drums, and that gave her an idea. "Hey, that'd be a cool name for a band," she said.

"Stuck In My Straw?" Sam asked.

Carly shook her head. "Strawberry Lumps."

Sam nodded in agreement. "Better."

"Hey, you got your drums all set up," Carly said to Spencer.

"Sort of," Spencer said. He noticed that fewer people came back from Groovy Smoothies than headed out a half an hour ago. "Where are Freddie and that girl, uh . . . ?" He couldn't remember her name, but he remembered her way too tight hugs.

"Mandy," Sam said with distaste.

"Freddie went home," Carly said.

"And we finally got rid of Mandy," Sam added.

Carly sighed. Mandy had barely stopped talking the entire time they were at Groovy Smoothies. "Someone needs to take that chick to the wacky shack."

"She lives here in Seattle?" Spencer asked. He put the snare drum back on its stand and started checking all the nuts and bolts to make sure they were tight enough.

"Nah, but way too close," Sam answered. Actually, anywhere on the planet Earth was too close when it came to Mandy.

87

"She's from Tacoma," Carly explained. "She made her aunt drive her all the way here so she could be on the show."

Sam was ready to stop talking about Mandy already. She hung her jacket on the coat rack. "Hey, can I spend the night here?" she asked.

"You don't want to go home?" Carly asked.

"Nah, when my mom buys a new bikini she usually wears it around for a couple of days to break it in." She put her hand on Carly's shoulder. "If you're my friend, you won't make me look at that," she joked.

Carly laughed. She was a good friend. She'd save Sam from the bikini if she could. "Can she spend the night?" Carly asked Spencer.

"Sure," Spencer said, tightening the last bolt. "Okay. All fixed, which means I'm now officially a drummer," he announced. He waved his drumsticks in the air and then hit them together a few times to set the beat. With a rock-and-roll flourish, he started pounding out a tune.

Carly and Sam cringed. They didn't want to insult Spencer or anything, but both of them were tempted to put their hands over their ears.

Spencer brought his drum solo to an end with a powerful hit on one of the cymbals.

It burst into flames.

"No!" Spencer yelled. He was totally bewildered. The drums weren't even connected to an electrical outlet. "How can that even happen?" he asked.

Carly ran for the fire extinguisher by the front door to put the flames out. *Poor Spencer*, she thought. Fire just seemed to follow him everywhere.

A couple of hours later, Carly and Sam had fallen asleep on the couch in front of the television. A loud cartoon woke Carly up and she nudged Sam.

"Sam." She let out a big yawn. "Sam," she said again. "We fell asleep."

Sam woke up with a groan. "Huh?" she asked.

"*Girlie Cow*'s on," Carly said.

Sam sat up with a yawn. "Oh, I love *Girlie Cow*." She watched the show for a minute. "Is this a new one?"

"I think," Carly said, rubbing her eyes.

They watched for a few seconds.

"Aw, cud! I can't believe two bulls asked me to the prom and I said moo to both," Girlie Cow said sadly. "Moo-hoo."

Carly and Sam heard a familiar nervous giggle and looked around. Mandy was sitting on the other end of the couch, eating popcorn, and laughing at the cartoon!

Carly jumped off the couch with a scream.

"Oh, I'm sorry, did I scare you guys?" Mandy asked.

"Yeah, kind of," Sam snarled.

"How'd you get in here?" Carly asked, totally shocked and surprised.

Sam was equally shocked. She had seen Mandy get into a car and drive away. Why was she back? "I thought you and your aunt left for Tacoma, like, four hours ago."

"We did, but you guys are so cool, I made my aunt get a room at a motel so I could spend the night here," Mandy explained. She ate some more popcorn. "Hey, remember on *iCarly* when you guys dressed that wiener dog up like a pig? Heh. Heh. That rocked."

Carly and Sam watched Mandy eat popcorn and exchanged horrified looks. The girl had somehow gotten into the apartment and had been sitting on the end of the couch while they slept. That was beyond creepy.

"How'd you get in here?" Carly asked again.

"The door was locked," Sam said.

"Yeah, but not all your windows were," Mandy said calmly. She ate some more popcorn. She was too excited to notice how horrified Carly and Sam were. "Hey, remember on *iCarly* when you guys put spaghetti in a blender? Heh. Heh. That was genius."

Carly was totally weirded out. "Thanks," she said carefully.

"Okay," Sam said slowly.

Mandy giggled again while Carly and Sam exchanged nervous smiles. She watched *Girlie Cow* for a few seconds and then pointed at the TV and laughed like a maniac.

Carly and Sam simply watched her. But that wasn't enough for Mandy. She wanted them to laugh at *Girlie Cow*, too. She threw handfuls of popcorn at them until they did the same.

Carly and Sam forced out a few awkward chuckles, but they were starting to get a little scared. Was their number one fan a crazy person? How would they ever get rid of her?

Chapter 4

A week later, Carly ran down the stairs between classes to look for Freddie and Sam. They were both in front of Freddie's locker. Mandy had finally gone back to Tacoma, but she made sure the *iCarly* team didn't forget her.

"Look," Carly said, showing them a greeting card. "I got another thank-you card from our biggest fan." She was totally exasperated. The cards were arriving every day, sometimes more than one at a time.

Sam and Freddie held up matching thank-you cards.

"You guys, too?" Carly asked.

Sam nodded. "Oh, not just another card." She pulled a boxed set of DVDs out of her backpack. "Mandy also sent me seasons one through four of *Girlie Cow* on DVD."

"She sent me a forty dollar gift card to Bandana Republic," Freddie said.

"Well, I got a new scarf and a box of frozen steaks," Carly told them.

Sam normally didn't complain about gifts, but Mandy was just too much. "When is she going to stop?"

"I don't know, it's been over a week," Carly said. "Do you know how many times she's text messaged me?" Her phone was getting so many texts that Carly was afraid it would stop working.

Sam was still thinking about the gifts. "Can I have the steaks?"

"What?" Carly yelled. They had a serious problem, and Sam was thinking about meat? They had to find a way to get Mandy to stop contacting them and sending them gifts.

Then, all of a sudden, their problem got worse — much worse.

Mandy ran down the hall toward them carrying books and wearing a backpack. "Hey, gang!" she said excitedly.

Carly jumped back. "Mandy!" She noticed that Mandy was wearing a Ridgeway sweatshirt with

the bulldog mascot. Ridgeway was Carly's school. The bulldog was her mascot. Not Mandy's. Or was it?

"Whoa," Sam said. She shot Carly and Freddie a look that said, "this is bad — this is really bad."

"Hi," Freddie said weakly.

Mandy bounced up and down with excitement. "Can you believe I'm here at Ridgeway?" she asked with a huge smile.

"No," Sam groaned.

"No, we can't," Freddie agreed, barely able to keep the dread out of his voice.

"It's true," Mandy said happily. "I'm officially a Bulldog." She opened her arms to show off her sweatshirt. "Woof!"

Carly tried to calm herself down. There must be a reasonable explanation. Mandy was just visiting or something. She tried to keep the fear out of her voice when she asked, "But why are you —"

Mandy cut her off. "I transferred schools!"

"You transferred schools?" Sam shouted. She turned to Carly and repeated it more quietly.

"She transferred schools." Her voice was full of anxiety.

"I heard her say she transferred schools," Carly said, just as anxiously.

"Now we can be together every day," Mandy said happily. "We'll be like the *iCarly* quartet. The two stars, the tech producer, and the show's biggest fan." Just in case they forgot who that was, Mandy pointed to herself and reminded them with a shout. "Me!"

The bell rang, which meant it was time for everybody to head to classes.

Mandy raced up the stairs, ready to be the best Ridgeway Bulldog she could possibly be.

Carly, Sam, and Freddie all stopped pretending to smile and let out huge groans. Carly dropped her face in her hands. Mandy would be around all the time now. It was too awful.

Then Sam remembered that the question she asked earlier hadn't been answered. "Seriously, can I have the steaks?"

Carly could only glare at her before heading off to history class.

Back at the loft, Spencer was frying a hamburger when the doorbell rang. He moved the pan off the burner and called out, running toward the door, "Here I come."

He opened the door to find a guy with spiky hair, lots of leather, and rings on every finger leaning up against the doorframe. A young woman stood behind him.

"Hey, so you must be Blake from the band," Spencer said.

"Yep. And I guess you're Poncy," Blake said.

"Spencer," Spencer answered, correcting him.

Blake pointed to the woman behind him. "This is my girlfriend and our keyboard player, Sue-zay," he said.

Spencer smiled and gave her a little wave. "Hi, Susie."

"Sue-zay," she said.

"Sue-zay?" Spencer asked, confused. Isn't that what he just said?

"It's not Susie," Blake said with a snarl.

"Sue-zay," the girl said again.

"Sue-zay," Spencer repeated.

Blake nodded. "Right."

Spencer opened the door wider. "Well, come on in," he said.

"Sure," Blake said.

Sue-zay was right behind him. "Thanks."

The two of them looked all around the apartment.

Spencer led them to his drums. "So, there's my drum set, right there," he said proudly.

Blake and Sue-zay checked out the drums.

Sue-zay wrinkled her nose. "Hey, these look just like the drums Kato threw out at the junkyard," she said.

"Weird!" Spencer said quickly. He didn't want Blake and Sue-zay to know that the junkyard was exactly where he got them, or that he had only been playing for a few days. "Weird coincidence." He changed the subject before they could look at the drums too closely. "Anyway, thanks for coming by. I guess you guys want to hear me play a little."

"Yeah, we can't really put you in the band till we hear you pound a little bit," Blake said.

98

"Oh, I'm ready to pound a little bit," Spencer said. "Or a lotta bit." He chuckled at his own joke, but Blake and Sue-zay only stared at him flatly.

Spencer quickly stopped chuckling and picked up his drumsticks. "I'll play the drums now," he said seriously.

Spencer had only been pounding on the drums for a few seconds when Blake and Sue-zay started to applaud.

"Wait, I was just getting started —" Spencer said.

Blake cut him off. "You're great," he said.

"Really?" Spencer asked. He couldn't believe it. He had only been playing for a couple of days and already he was great!

"Yeah, you're super-drummy," Blake said, giving him a thumbs-up.

"Thanks! So, can I be in the band or what?" Spencer asked.

"Will you answer one very important question?" Blake asked.

Suddenly Spencer was afraid he wouldn't be able to answer the question. He was especially

bad at answering questions about Canada. "Does it involve Canadian trivia?"

Blake looked confused for a moment. "No."

"Then I will answer this question," Spencer said solemnly.

"Can we use this apartment to rehearse whenever we want?" Blake asked.

"Sure," Spencer said.

Blake reached out to shake his hand. "Then congratulations, Alfonzo."

"Spencer," he said, taking Blake's hand.

"You're in the band," Blake said.

Spencer jumped to his feet. "Yes!" he shouted, and then pulled Blake into a Mandy-like bear hug and lifted him into the air. "Thank you so much!"

Spencer couldn't believe how lucky he was. He was going to be a drummer in a rock-and-roll band!

After school that day, Carly, Sam, and Freddie rushed into the loft and slammed the door behind them. Sam made sure the dead bolt was locked. Freddie slid the chain lock into place.

100

"There," Sam said.

"We're safe," Freddie added.

Carly breathed a huge sigh of relief. No Mandy in sight.

Spencer was sitting behind his drums. "What happened?" he asked.

"Mandy happened," Carly said.

"I thought she went back to Tacoma," Spencer said.

"Yeah, and then she transferred to our school," Carly said, totally annoyed.

Freddie poured himself a glass of iced tea. "Mandy's nuts, dude, the girl is nuts," he yelled.

Carly threw her backpack on the couch. Every time she turned around at school, she bumped right into Mandy. "She asked if she could do her impression of a duck, then quacked right in my face. Quacked right in it!" she yelled.

"Can't you guys just tell her to leave you alone?" Spencer asked.

"We tried," Freddie told him.

Sam threw her arms up in the air in exasperation. "She won't listen."

"She tried to follow us home!" Carly yelled. "I

had to get rid of her by telling her we need some Fladoodles for the show."

Now Spencer was even more confused. "What are Fladoodles?"

"I don't know," Carly admitted. "I made them up."

Suddenly Freddie noticed that Spencer's drums didn't look like a junkyard find anymore. They were bright red and shiny instead of silver and dull. "Are those new drums?"

"Oh, yeah! I didn't tell you guys. I auditioned and I got in the band," Spencer said.

Carly tried to be happy for him, despite her Mandy problem. "Cool."

So did Sam and Freddie. "Nice going," they said.

"Thanks. And that old drum set was jank so I figured I'd just spend the bucks and get myself these." Spencer patted a drum and then picked up his sticks. "You want to hear how they sound?" he asked.

Carly and her friends were about to say yes when they heard someone wriggle the knob and then knock on the door.

"It's *meeeeee!*" Mandy shouted.

Carly cringed. "Aw, man," she said.

Sam couldn't believe it. They had sent Mandy out on an errand to find something that didn't even exist just a few minutes ago. "How can Mandy be back here already?" she asked.

Carly shrugged and opened the door with a sigh. Mandy stood there with a snack bag of Fladoodles in one hand and a full supermarket bag in the other.

"I found Fladoodles," she said with a big smile. She shook the bag in Carly's face.

Carly and her friends were totally blown away. They hadn't realized that Fladoodles were real.

"I thought they didn't exist," Sam said.

Mandy looked at her suspiciously.

Carly elbowed Sam in the side. "She means we thought they'd be really hard to find."

"Oh, they were," Mandy assured her. "I had to try seven different places, until I finally found them in this weird Scandinavian market in Nordic Town." She handed the bag to Carly. "Here you go!"

Carly didn't even know Seattle had a Nordic Town. Mandy had lived here for a day and had

already found it. She took the Fladoodles bag from her number one fan with a weak smile.

"Thanks," Sam said with a groan.

Freddie forced himself to smile. "Great."

Carly looked at the bag and got an idea. "But we needed fat-free Fladoodles," she said.

Mandy reached into her supermarket bag and whipped out fat-free Fladoodles. "Fat-free!" she said with a happy giggle. "I also have barbecue, cool ranch, and zesty jalapeno. Heh. Heh."

The entire *iCarly* team flinched. They were stuck with Mandy. Maybe forever.

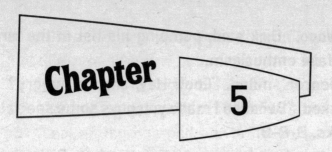

Chapter 5

The next day, while Carly was trying to dodge Mandy and her duck impressions at school, Spencer had his first band practice. Blake and Sue-zay came over with Dirk, their bass player. Spencer had dressed up in what he thought was his coolest, his most rock-and-roll outfit — black leather pants and a sleeveless T-shirt with red stripes to match his drums. He wore a terrycloth headband and wrist guards. The whole effect was more goofball than rock-and-roll.

Spencer pounded on his drums, totally offbeat. The rest of the band finished their first song long before he did, so he hit the cymbal a few times for good measure. He was totally psyched. "How was that?" he asked.

"Great," Blake lied.

Sue-zay nodded. "Smokin'."

"Wooo," Dirk said, pumping his fist in the air with fake enthusiasm.

Spencer smiled. "Cool! Hey, anyone hungry?" he asked. "Because I made you guys some special snacks. B-R-B."

As soon as he was out of earshot, Dirk and Sue-zay walked over to Blake.

"Look, man, that dude drums like puke," Dirk said.

Sue-zay crossed her arms over her chest with a determined expression. "How long are we going to pretend he's in the band?" she demanded.

"C'mon, he's making us snacks," Blake said.

"Snacks?" Dirk shook his head. "It ain't worth it."

"Seriously. He can't play," Sue-zay added.

Blake sighed. Sue-zay and Dirk were right. They were just using Spencer because they needed a place to rehearse and a set of drums, but Spencer was so bad that they'd be better off not rehearsing at all. "All right," he agreed. "Let's just kick him out now then."

"Good," Sue-zay said.

Dirk nodded. "About time."

Something beeped in the kitchen. Spencer checked his cell and ran into the living room with a plate of deviled eggs. "I hope you guys like deviled eggs — and good news!" he said.

Blake grabbed an egg. "Good news?"

"Are you ready?" Spencer asked. "Okay, what would you say if I told you —" Spencer paused dramatically and made sure all three of his band-mates were listening carefully. "I booked our band on *Seattle Beat*?"

Blake's jaw dropped. "What?" he asked.

Sue-zay and Dirk were totally surprised. *Seattle Beat* was one of their favorite television shows. All the cool Seattle bands appeared on the music show. Teens hung outside the show's big windows every day so that they could see their favorite local bands up close and personal — and get their pictures on TV.

"*Seattle Beat*?" Sue-zay asked.

"No way!" Dirk said.

"Uh-huh," Spencer told them, totally enjoying the moment. "My buddy Socko knows their talent booker, so I emailed him a couple of your songs, and we are booked on the show for next Friday," Spencer explained.

"That's awesome!" Dirk said.

Blake and Sue-zay bumped fists.

Spencer raised his hand for a high-five, but everyone ignored him.

"We've been trying to get booked on *Seattle Beat* for three years!" Sue-zay said.

"So," Blake said, giving Sue-zay and Dirk a meaningful look, "you guys wanted to tell him something?"

There was no way they wanted to kick Spencer out of the band now — not without losing their spot on *Seattle Beat*.

"We're just psyched to have you as our drummer," Sue-zay lied.

Dirk smiled. "Glad you're in the band, dude."

"Yeah!" Spencer yelled. He grabbed his drumsticks and sat behind his instrument. "Let's play it up!" he shouted.

The rest of the band winced as they started to play. Spencer's drumming was worse than bad. It was completely dreadful.

That night, Carly and Sam were getting ready to start their Webcast. Freddie was at his tech station, making sure that everything was ready to go. Mandy, unfortunately, was smiling big from the middle of Spencer's seat sculpture. She had insisted on being their live audience of one again.

Freddie picked up his handheld camera. "All right, in five, four, three, two . . ." On one the red light on his camera blinked on and he pointed to Sam and Carly. . . .

"And now . . ." Carly said, smiling big for the camera.

"Webcasting to you live from Seattle . . ." Sam added.

"My name's Carly," Carly said.

"And my name's Sam."

Suddenly, Mandy wasn't in her seat anymore. She poked her head up between Carly and Sam. "And my name's Mandy!" she shouted with a laugh.

Carly and Sam wanted to push her right out of

the shot, but they couldn't — not on a live Webcast. What would their other fans think?

"Yes, you remember Mandy," Carly said with an awkward smile.

"Our audience member from last week," Sam explained to the camera.

"Who's still here," Carly said.

Mandy waved to the *iCarly* viewers.

"And is supposed to be sitting quietly in her seat over there," Sam said pointedly, from between clenched teeth.

"Ooo, right. Sorry. Heh. Heh," Mandy said. She looked into the camera again. "Go *iCarly*!" she shouted, and then ran back to her seat.

Carly was relieved to have the Webcast under control again. "Okay, tonight we're going to kick off the show with one of your favorites," she said.

"'Messin' with Lewbert!'" she and Sam both said together. A graphic appeared on the screen as they said it.

Sam pushed the button on her remote control that filled the studio with cheers and applause.

Lewbert was Carly's super-mean doorman. Her viewers couldn't get enough of the Lewbert

segments, especially when the *iCarly* team tricked him and secretly caught the action on a hidden Lewbert-cam. And then there was Lewbert's wart — it was enormous and right in the middle of his cheek! It was ghastly. It was repulsive. And their audience absolutely loved it.

"We're about to play the best trick ever on my horrible doorman," Carly said.

"Who may be the most disgusting dude in all of doormanity," Sam added, making up a word.

Sam would have said more, but at that moment Mandy popped up between Carly and Sam again. This time she was wearing a duck mask. She made some quacking sounds right in front of the camera and then in Sam and Carly's faces. She raised the duck mask with a giggle so they could see who she was — as if they didn't know — and then turned back to the camera, sticking her face right in front of the lens.

"That was my impression of a duck." Mandy giggled some more. "Here it comes again!" Mandy happily pulled the mask over her face and started to quack.

Carly gave her viewers a weak smile. "Yes, quack, quack," she said.

All Carly and Sam could do was stare into the camera. *Forget about 'Messin' with Lewbert,'* they thought. Mandy was messin' with them.

Chapter 6

The next day, Carly came home from school to find Spencer slumped on the couch clutching a pillow. His band's CD played quietly in the background.

"Hey," Carly said.

"Hey," Spencer said with a sad expression.

"What's wrong?" Carly asked.

Spencer handed her a piece of paper to explain.

"Who's this from?" Carly asked.

"My band," Spencer said. He used the remote to turn down the music. "Read it out loud."

"'Dear Splinter,'" Carly said.

Spencer sighed. "He never did learn my name."

Carly kept reading. "'Thanks for getting us booked on *Seattle Beat*. You rock for that. Unfortunately, your drumming is suckish.'" Carly

took in Spencer's sad expression. She knew how psyched he had been about being in a band. "Aww," she said sympathetically.

"That's where I said aww, too," Spencer said. He motioned to Carly to keep reading.

"'So we've decided to go ahead with our appearance on *Seattle Beat*, but we're kicking you out of the band,'" Carly read. "'Also, we took the rest of the deviled eggs and stole your drums. Take care, Blake.'" Carly looked up from the note. "Well, that wasn't nice at all," she said.

Spencer buried his face in the pillow. "Nope," he mumbled.

Carly rubbed her brother's head. "I'm sorry."

"Thanks," Spencer said. "I've just been sitting here, listening to their music."

"Well, don't do that. They're mean people," Carly told him.

"I know," Spencer said. His face crumpled, and he looked like he might cry. He buried his face in the pillow again. "But their music is so good. They took my drums!" he moaned.

There was a knock on the door and Sam and Freddie came in.

"Hey," Sam said.

"You ready?" Freddie asked.

"Yeah," Carly told them. She turned to Spencer. "We're going to go upstairs and jam on more ideas for *iCarly* before Mandy shows up."

"Okay," Spencer said. He dragged himself to his feet and headed for the front door. "I'm going to go for a walk," he said sadly.

"Take an umbrella," Carly said.

Spencer looked like a sad little boy. "I don't want to," he whined, and trudged out into the hall without one.

"Why's he all sad?" Freddie asked.

Carly didn't want to go into it right then. There was too much work to do before Mandy arrived uninvited and ruined their afternoon. "I'll tell you later. Let's get upstairs before you-know-who shows up."

"Yeah," Sam agreed.

"Okay," Freddie said.

Carly and her friends ran upstairs seconds before Mandy burst through the front door.

"Carly?" she called. "You home from school yet? Freddie?" Mandy looked around. She heard

115

the music playing quietly in the background and spotted the remote. She turned it up and started dancing to the song. "This music is fantastic," she said. "Yeah!" She pumped her arms and moved her legs to the rhythm. "Rock it, baby!"

The CD case was sitting on the coffee table next to the remote. She picked it up and started to read. It told Mandy all she needed to know about her new favorite band.

A few hours later, Carly and Sam had almost reached the end of their Webcast and Mandy still hadn't appeared. They were so grateful not to have to listen to her quacking noises that they didn't even wonder about what might have happened to her.

They were in the middle of a classic *iCarly* moment. Freddie had somehow managed to get a close-up photo of an actor's hairy armpit. They displayed it for their viewers.

Freddie pulled back from the image on the monitor and focused on Carly and Sam.

Carly brought the segment to an end. "And that was this week's . . ."

". . . celebrity armpit," Sam finished, pushing the applause button on her remote.

Carly looked into the camera. "Okay, now . . ." she said.

Sam took over to begin the next segment. ". . . to conclude this fine Webcast."

Carly picked up a glass of water. "Sam and I will demonstrate the classic comedy bit called The Spit Take."

Carly started to drink her glass of water.

"Hey, Carly, remember at lunch when you asked me to put ketchup on your fries?" Sam asked.

"Mmm-hmm," Carly answered, still drinking.

"It was really chicken blood," Sam said with a straight face.

Carly spit out her water, spraying it all over the studio. She laughed. "And that's what's known as . . ."

"The Spit Take," she and Sam sang in unison. A graphic appeared on the screen under their faces, with drops of water falling off the letters.

Carly laughed. "Okay, check us out next week . . ."

". . . here at iCarly-dot-com," Sam said.

117

Together, the girls said good-bye to their viewers. "Ciao! Buh-*byeeee!*"

"Keep clicking away," Sam added.

Freddie typed a command into his laptop and brought the show to a close. "*Aaaannndddd . . .* we're clear."

"Woo-hoo!" Carly yelled.

"Yeah!" Sam pumped her fist in the air.

"Awesome show, you guys," Freddie said.

"You, too," Carly told him.

"Agreed," Sam said.

Freddie picked up three stem glasses with fancy umbrellas in them. "And now, some punch for you," he said handing one to Carly. "For you," he said to Sam. "And for me!"

He raised his glass high. "To Mandy," he toasted. "Who knows what happened to her?"

"Let's just be psyched that she's out of our lives," Carly said, clinking glasses with her friends.

"Awesome spit take by the way," Freddie told her.

"Yeah, it felt good," Carly joked.

Carly blanched when she heard heavy foot-steps racing up the stairs. Was Mandy back? Then she heard her brother calling her name and she relaxed again.

"Carly!" he yelled. "Guys! Carly! Hey!" Spencer was so out of breath that he could hardly talk. "You guys . . ." he huffed.

"What?" Carly asked.

Freddie put his punch down. "Are you okay?"

"What's up?" Sam asked.

"Turn on the TV," Spencer said, huffing and puffing. "Channel seven!"

"Why?" Freddie asked.

"Just turn it on!" Carly urged.

"Okay, okay!" Freddie scrambled to his tech station and activated the TV monitor. It swung out from its position on the wall.

"What's on?" Sam asked.

"*Seattle Beat*. I turned it on to see if the band was using my stolen drums — they were — and right in the middle of their song —"

Freddie cut Spencer off. "Here, I got it," he said, using the remote to change the channel.

There on the screen, they saw Spencer's old band. But standing right in the middle of Blake, Sue-zay, Dirk, and the new drummer was *iCarly*'s old number one fan, Mandy! She was giggling and waving at the camera.

Someone who worked at the station was trying to get her off the stage. "Off! Get off the stage!" he yelled in a loud whisper.

Freddie's jaw dropped. He pointed to the screen. "That's Mandy!"

"Oh my gosh," Sam said slowly.

Carly cracked up. "This is too great."

Mandy was talking to the camera. "People of Seattle, this is the best band ever!" she squealed. Then she turned to Blake. "I am your guys' biggest fan in the whole wide world! Heh. Heh."

Blake looked completely horrified. Mandy was not the kind of fan he and his band had in mind.

Mandy didn't notice. She was carrying a tray of cookies. "Look, I made you guys cookies with your faces on them. See?" Mandy held her cookies up to the camera. "Here's Blake, Dirk, and Susie."

"Sue-zay!" Sue-zay snapped at her.

The producers were still trying to get Mandy off the stage so that the band could play their music, but she completely ignored them. "I'm going to hang out with you guys all the time!" she told the band happily. Then she launched herself at Blake and gave him a super-tight bear hug.

Offstage, Carly and her friends could hear a *Seattle Beat* producer yelling, "Somebody call the cops!"

Mandy was oblivious. She put on her duck mask and started quacking at the camera and then at each band member. No one knew quite what to do with her. Blake could only watch in horror, and Sue-zay was still furious that Mandy had gotten her name wrong.

Mandy lifted her mask for a moment and laughed at the camera. "Here it comes again," she said, pulling the duck's bill over her mouth. "Quack, quack! Quack, quack!"

Spencer laughed for the first time since he had gotten Blake's note. "Woo, go Mandy!" he said, clapping.

Carly and her friends applauded too.

"Go, girl!" Freddie cheered.

"Yeah, Mandy!" Sam said.

Carly laughed. Having an over-the-top, irritating, obsessive fan like Mandy was exactly what that band deserved for stealing Spencer's drums. Life was sweet!